Encourage and inspire women to believe, have hope, and STAY STRONG!

#EmbracingthePowerInMe

To Jhilyn, my miracle child who I was able to carry for nine months and experience giving birth to, and to J2. Without you both, I would not be a mother.

To Jhilyn's godmother and my good friend, Mariel, who has provided me with emotional support to push through and not give up on myself.

To my partner, James, who somehow managed to be patient, understanding, and supportive through my journey.

To the mother that raised James, my future mother-in-law, Terry Lynn, who I never got to meet, and who passed on December 18, 2015, from breast cancer. I was told she was strong, a fighter, and all about family!

To my parents, who sacrificed everything to ensure my siblings and I got what we needed in life. For my dad, Yen Thach, who inspires me every day to fight and stay strong, and who passed on January 17, 2021.

And for all the women who are fighting cancer.

www.mascotbooks.com

Momma Has Cancer

©2023 Phi Thach. All Rights Reserved. No part of this publication may be reproduced, stored in a retrieval system or transmitted in any form by any means electronic, mechanical, or photocopying, recording or otherwise without the permission of the author.

For more information, please contact:
Mascot Kids, an imprint of Amplify Publishing Group
620 Herndon Parkway, Suite 320
Herndon, VA 20170
info@mascotbooks.com

Library of Congress Control Number: 2022909283

CPSIA Code: PRT0722A
ISBN-13: 978-1-63755-379-4

Printed in the United States

Momma has cancer ... the church prays for YOU.

Momma has cancer ... don't let that discourage YOU.

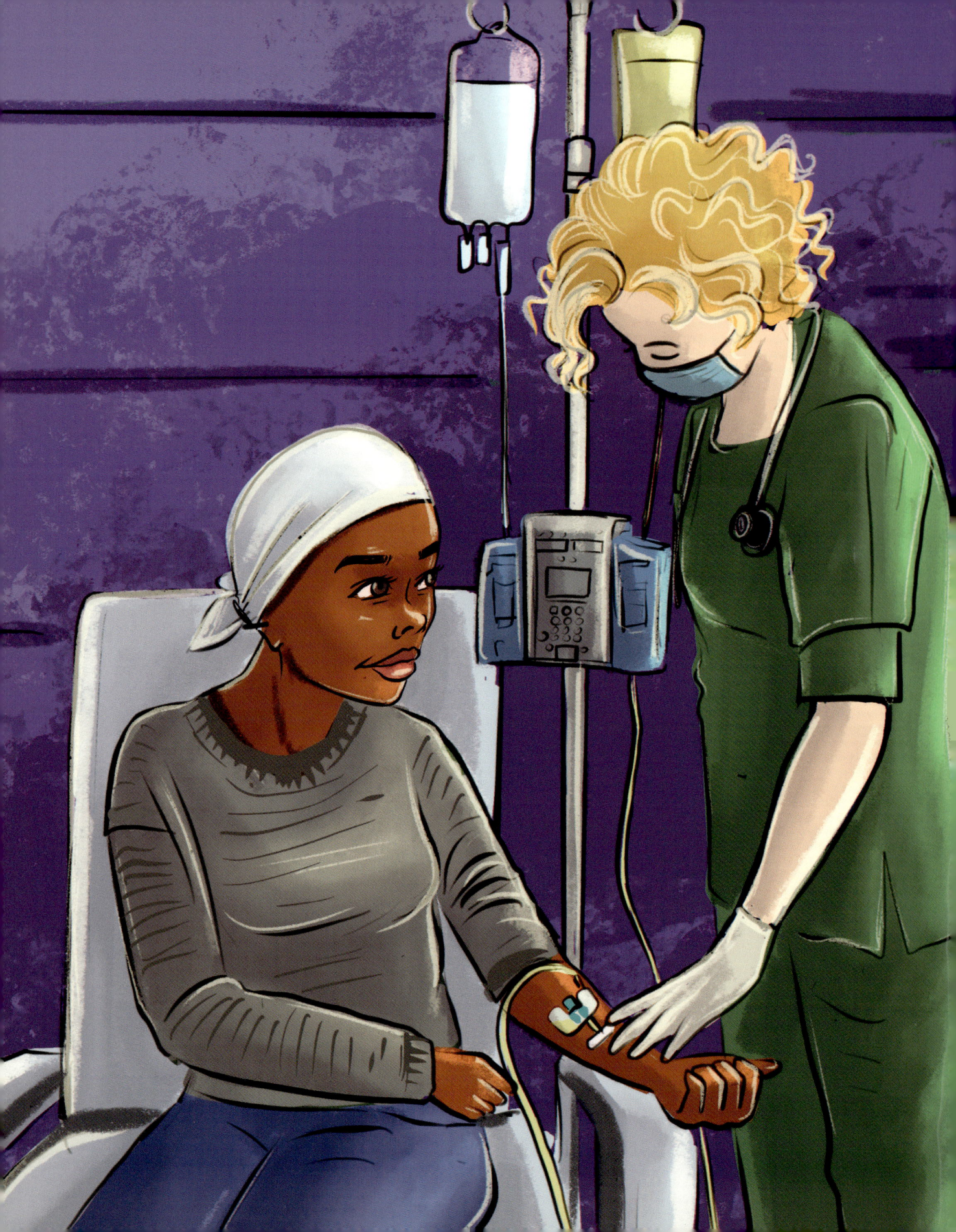

Momma has cancer . . . and will fight to make it THROUGH.

Momma wants you to know . . . people in our world will have their own VIEWS.

Momma has cancer . . . and still believes in YOU.

Momma has cancer ... who would have KNOWN.

Momma has cancer . . . and still prays for YOU.

Momma had cancer . . .

and gave birth to YOU!

About the Author

Phi T. Thach was born in the Philippines. Her mother is from Cambodia, and her father is from Vietnam. After Phi's mother escaped Cambodia and her father escaped as a prisoner of war from Vietnam, Phi's parents met in Thailand and later moved to the Philippines, where they had Phi. They then immigrated to the United States and settled in Silver Spring, Maryland, where Phi grew up. She remembers watching her father advocate for the people in his community, which initiated her journey to find her purpose in life. Phi received her associate's degree in business administration, her bachelor's degree in social work, and a master's degree in early childhood education. She's continuing her education and working towards her doctorate degree in human services, specializing in leadership and organizational management.

Phi currently works as a community schools coordinator. In this role, Phi is able to work on creating promising partnerships, securing grants and sponsorships, and advocating for mental health services, efficient housing, healthier food, and employment for newly migrated families. Phi is dedicated and committed to improving behavioral and academic needs for youth, families, and communities by providing resources and support, addressing and capitalizing on individual strengths, and guiding families in their development and achievement of academic and personal goals. Phi visualizes a world filled with youth who truly believe they can achieve anything, and she has dedicated her career to ensuring they have the tools to do so.

In August 2015, Phi was diagnosed with stage 3 cervical cancer and went through chemo and radiation therapy. Doctors told her it was possible that she would be unable to have children. This news was devastating for her, as she loves to work with children and always wanted her own. When she found out she was pregnant in January 2019, she was so excited! Her son, Jhilyn, inspired her to write *Momma Has Cancer*. She wants to share with her son the emotions that she endured and the strength she had to discover to overcome them.

For press inquiries, please email careertoolkitsbydee@gmail.com, and for social media management requests, please message @careertoolkitsbydee on Instagram.